A Note to Parents and Teachers

DK READERS is a compelling program for beginning readers, designed in conjunction with leading literacy experts, including Dr. Linda Gambrell, Professor of Education at Clemson University. Dr. Gambrell has served as President of the National Reading Conference and the College Reading Association, and is the current President of the International Reading Association (2007–2008.)

Beautiful illustrations and superb full-color photographs combine with engaging, easy-to-read text to offer a fresh approach to each subject in the series. Each DK READER is guaranteed to capture a child's interest while developing his or her reading skills, general knowledge, and love of reading.

The five levels of DK READERS are aimed at different reading abilities, enabling you to choose the books that are exactly right for your child:

Pre-level 1: Learning to read
Level 1: Beginning to read
Level 2: Beginning to read alone
Level 3: Reading alone
Level 4: Proficient readers

The "normal" age at which a child begins to read can be anywhere from three to eight years old, so these levels are only a general guideline.

No matter which level you select, you can be sure that you are helping your child learn to read, then read to learn!

LONDON, NEW YORK, MUNICH,
MELBOURNE, AND DELHI

Senior Editor Catherine Saunders
Designer Jon Hall
Brand Manager Robert Perry
Publishing Manager Simon Beecroft
Category Publisher Siobhan Williamson
Production Editor Hitesh Patel
Production Amy Bennett

Reading Consultant
Linda Gambrell

First published in the United States in 2007 by
DK Publishing
375 Hudson Street
New York, New York 10014

07 08 09 10 11 10 9 8 7 6 5 4 3 2 1
MD413—10/07

DK books are available at special discounts when purchased in bulk for
sales promotions, premiums, fund-raising, or educational use.
For details contact: DK Publishing Special Markets
375 Hudson Street
New York, New York 10014
SpecialSales@dk.com

A catalog record for this book is available from the Library of Congress.

ISBN 978-0-7566-3494-0 (paperback)
ISBN 978-0-7566-3495-7 (hardback)

Color reproduction by GRB Editrice S.r.l., London
Printed and bound by L-Rex, China.

Discover more at
www.dk.com

Contents

DK READERS

MARVEL HEROES

AMAZING POWERS

READING
3
ALONE

Written by Catherine Saunders

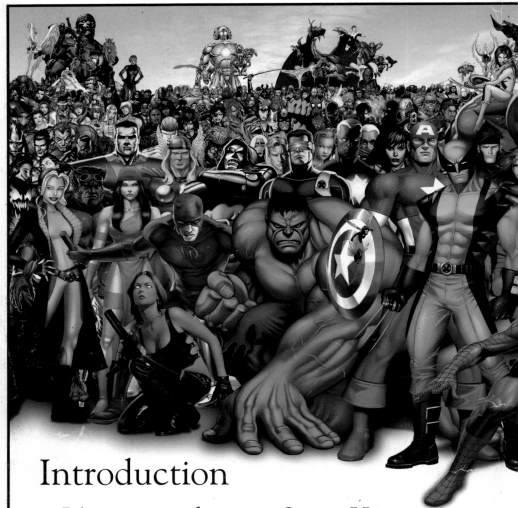

Introduction

It's not easy being a Super Hero. It takes great courage for a hero to put his or her life on the line to fight evil villains and defend innocent people. But Super Heroes are men, women, and creatures with extraordinary abilities.

Read on and meet some of the bravest Super Heroes around. Discover how they got their amazing powers and find out how they put them into action! But beware, evil Super Villains are always lurking just around the corner...

The Amazing Spider-Man

Spider-Man is the secret Super Hero identity of high school student Peter Parker. While Peter Parker is shy, nerdy, and not very strong, Spider-Man is the complete opposite. Spider-Man is strong, fast, agile, and not afraid to take on bad guys.

Spider-Man swings through the air on his web.

Spider-Man can climb the tallest buildings.

Spider sense warns Spidey of approaching danger.

Like a spider, he can stick to almost any surface which means Spider-Man is great at climbing walls and tall buildings! However, Peter Parker's brains are also useful for Spider-Man, and it was thanks to his brilliance that Spidey developed the ability to shoot webs from his wrists.

Amazing Accident
Peter Parker wasn't born with his amazing powers. His life changed when he was bitten by a radioactive spider on a trip to a science exhibition.

Fantastic Friends

Although he usually works alone, sometimes even Spider-Man needs a little help. The Super Hero team known as the Fantastic Four are some of his greatest allies. The Fantastic Four are Mr. Fantastic; his wife, the Invisible Woman; her brother, the Human Torch; and finally the rock-hard Thing. Like Spider-Man, the Fantastic Four were not born with their powers. During a space mission, the team were exposed to cosmic radiation, which mutated their bodies.

Best Buddies
Spidey has a lot in common with the Human Torch and the two Super Heroes have become friends. Villains had better watch out with this pair on their tail!

Mr. Fantastic

Even before he was transformed into Mr. Fantastic, Reed Richards was a special person. He was a respected inventor and scientific genius. One of his most ambitious projects was building a starship, but little did he imagine that his dream of exploring the stars would lead him to develop super powers. After his exposure to cosmic radiation, Reed developed elastic abilities.

Reed Richards likes to stretch the boundaries of science!

Mr. Fantastic can flatten his body so that it is as thin as paper or stretch it up to 1500 feet long. He can bend his body into useful shapes such as a parachute or a tent, and it doesn't hurt a bit! However, Mr. Fantastic may have Super Hero stretching powers but he only has the strength of an ordinary man.

Stretching the Imagination
Mr. Fantastic has also found his super powers very useful for his experiments. He can work faster and reach further—in fact he's more than twice the man he used to be!

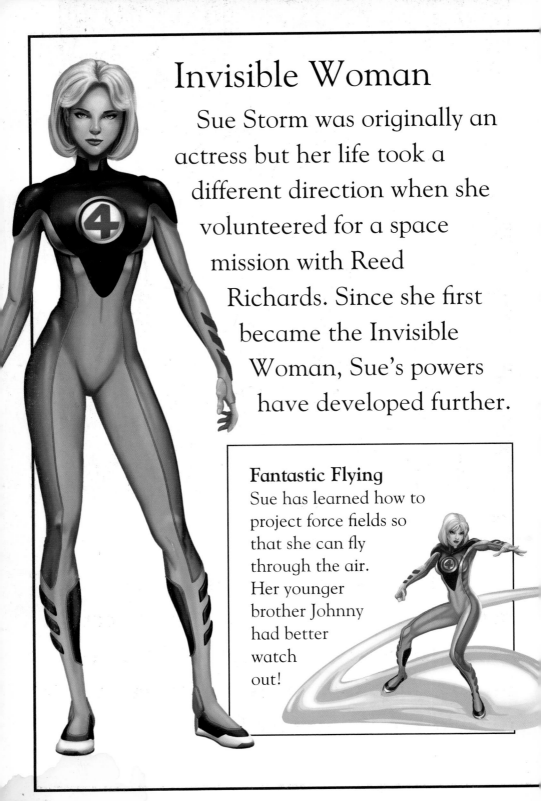

Invisible Woman

Sue Storm was originally an actress but her life took a different direction when she volunteered for a space mission with Reed Richards. Since she first became the Invisible Woman, Sue's powers have developed further.

Fantastic Flying
Sue has learned how to project force fields so that she can fly through the air. Her younger brother Johnny had better watch out!

*Sue has learned how
to use her abilities to project force fields.*

These days she can not only make
herself invisible, but she can also project
energy to make other people and objects
invisible too. Sue can also project energy
to make protective force fields.

The Human Torch

Little did Johnny Storm know that visiting his big sister would change his life! When he returned from that fateful space mission, Johnny discovered that the cosmic rays had altered his genetic structure. He can now generate a fiery plasma which covers his entire body, without so much as singeing a hair. As the Human Torch, Johnny can fly and he can also release a burst of energy with as much force as a nuclear weapon.

Hot Stuff

Johnny can manipulate the flames to create any shape. Although the powerful flames do not harm Johnny's body, his clothes are not so lucky! These days all his clothes have to be made from special flame-resistant fabric.

Watch out! The Thing is coming!

The Thing

Sports-loving Ben Grimm met brilliant scientist Reed Richards at university and the mis-matched pair soon became best friends. After college, Ben joined the US Air Force and became a pilot.

So when Reed started planning a mission into space, Ben was the obvious choice to pilot his space craft. After the disastrous mission, Ben was transformed into The Thing—a creature with super human strength and endurance. Although his rock hard exterior can withstand bullets, extreme temperatures, the depths of the ocean, and even space travel, The Thing has a very kind heart.

The X-Men

The X-Men are a team of Super Hero mutants. Mutants are humans who have been born with special abilities such as superhuman strength or the power to control the weather. The X-Men were brought together by Professor Charles Xavier.

According to Professor Xavier the "X" stands for the "extra" powers that mutants have. Many humans fear the X-Men because of their extraordinary abilities so Professor Xavier wants to teach them how best to use their super powers. The X-Men have some powerful enemies, including the evil mutant Magneto. Thankfully, the X-Men also have many Super Hero friends, such as Spider-Man, the Fantastic Four and the Avengers.

Professor Charles Xavier
The founder of the X-Men is a mutant whose super power is telepathy. When he was a young man, Professor Xavier lost the use of his legs after a battle with an alien called Lucifer. He has been confined to a wheelchair ever since.

Wolverine

Wolverine was a loner until he met Professor Xavier and became one of the X-Men. Wolverine was born with razor sharp claws made of bone and he has the power to heal any wound almost instantly. Wolverine's powers became even greater when he was forced to take part in a secret government experiment. In order to create a "super soldier" Wolverine's skeleton was coated with a virtually unbreakable metal called adamantium.

Adamantium Skeleton
Thanks to their adamantium coating, Wolverine's claws can slice through almost anything. The claws are retractable which means that he can sheath and unsheath them whenever he likes.

Jean Grey

Jean Grey was one of the original members of the X-Men team. Like Professor Xavier, Jean has the power of telepathy, which means that she can read other people's thoughts and feelings.

Jean first met Professor Xavier when she was just eleven years old. The Professor helped Jean to control her powerful telepathic abilities until she was old enough to use them safely.

The Professor also helped the young Jean to develop a new power—telekinesis. Telekinesis is the power to move and control objects with your mind.

At first Jean Grey's X-Men code name was Marvel Girl but she later became known as Phoenix. Jean has a romantic relationship with another of the original X-Men—Scott Summers, who is also known as Cyclops.

Phoenix

When Jean Grey was exposed to solar radiation, her dying body was invaded by a powerful cosmic entity called the Phoenix Force. The Phoenix Force had the power to surround Jean's body with a fiery bird shape. The other X-Men believed that Phoenix was the real Jean Grey.

Rogue

Rogue is a mutant with the power to absorb the memories, abilities, and personality of anyone she touches. Rogue first discovered her powers when she kissed her friend Cody Robbins and absorbed his memories. Frightened by her powers, she turned to the X-Men for help.

Rogue wears gloves to protect other people from her powers.

Storm

Orphan Ororo Monroe grew up in Africa. Her mutant ability to control the weather meant that she was worshipped as a goddess by some tribes. Professor Xavier traveled to Africa to convince Ororo to use her powers to help humanity instead. Ororo agreed and joined the the X-Men, where she adopted the code name Storm.

Weather Warning
Storm has the power to control the rain, snow, sleet, fog, and hail. She can summon lightning in an instant, create a hurricane, or lower the temperature to freezing point.

Nightcrawler

Kurt Wagner has three fingers on each hand, two toes on each foot, a tail, pointed ears, yellow eyes, and indigo skin. He is the son of an evil shape-shifting mutant called Mystique and a German baron. He has the mutant ability to teleport and is one of the X-Men.

Kurt's X-Men code name is Nightcrawler.

Cyclops

Scott Summers was the first member of the X-Men. Known as Cyclops, Scott is able to absorb sunlight and project beams of solar energy from his eyes. These beams are strong enough to blast holes through a mountain. Unfortunately, Scott cannot control the beams because of a childhood brain injury, so he must always wear glasses or a visor. If Cyclops did not wear eye protection, he would simply blast everyone and everything he sees!

Cyclops often leads the X-Men.

The Hulk

When scientist Bruce Banner was caught in the blast from a gamma radiation bomb, it unleashed a whole different side to his personality. From then on, whenever Bruce becomes stressed or angry he transforms into the raging, unstoppable—and green— Incredible Hulk. Although his great powers make him very destructive, the Hulk really just wants to be left alone.

Super-Strength
Rage combined with gamma radiation give the Hulk almost unlimited strength. His powerful legs can jump several miles and he can also heal any wound almost instantly. The Hulk can even withstand bullets.

Hulk and Wolverine

These two powerful Super Heroes have a lot in common, although they might not like to admit it! Both Hulk and Wolverine are fearsome tough guys with awesome strength and the ability to heal themselves.

Although Wolverine was born with amazing powers and Hulk acquired his after an accident, they both find it hard to deal with being a Super Hero and often prefer to be alone. Luckily Wolverine has finally found some Super Hero friends in the X-Men, but, despite a short time in the Avengers, Hulk still wanders alone.

Hulk's massive frame would strike fear into the hearts of any villain, while few evil-doers would be a match for Wolverine's claws. If these two loners ever decide to team up, the world had better watch out!

The Avengers

A Super Hero team called the Avengers was brought together to defeat villains too powerful for a lone hero. The team was formed when God of Evil, Loki, tried to take revenge on his half brother, Thor. Loki tricked Hulk into causing a train wreck, in the hope of trapping Thor. But instead, several heroes arrived to fight poor Hulk. The group included Ant-Man, Wasp, and Iron Man, as well as Thor. When they had defeated Loki, Ant Man suggested that they form a permanent Super Hero team.

New Recruits
The Avengers' line up is always changing. The Avengers rescued Captain America and then asked him to join the team. Spidey is also a new recruit.

Captain America

Steve Rogers wanted to join the US Army and fight in World War II, but he was turned down because he was too weak. However, when he volunteered to test the Super-Soldier Serum, Steve's body underwent an amazing transformation. It virtually doubled in size, turning Steve from a frail man to near physically perfect Super Hero with the ability to lift twice his own weight.

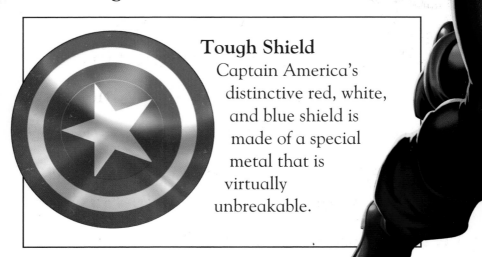

Tough Shield
Captain America's distinctive red, white, and blue shield is made of a special metal that is virtually unbreakable.

Now known as Captain America, Steve trained in martial arts, gymnastics, and military tactics. The red, white, and blue hero has sworn to uphold freedom and democracy, either alone or with Super Hero friends such as the Avengers.

Iron Man

Iron Man is the Super Hero alter ego of billionaire businessman, Tony Stark. Iron Man has superhuman strength and durability, thanks to his specially developed protective armor.

At first Stark only used Iron Man to deal with threats to his business empire but he later realized that his Super Hero persona could be put to better use. Iron Man became one of the founder members of the Super Hero team, the Avengers.

Weapons
Iron Man's armor has many state-of-the-art features. These include jet-propelled boots, gauntlets with repulsor beams, and a chest mounted uni beam.

Thor

Thor is the Norse God of Thunder. His father Odin sent him to Earth to become more humble. But it's hard to be humble if you have awesome strength and are almost impossible to beat in a fight! Like Iron Man, Thor is a founding member of the Avengers.

Thor's hammer also helps him to fly.

Thor's Hammer
Thor wields the hammer of Mjolnir. Not only is it unbreakable, but it can also fire energy blasts, channel storms, and open interdimensional portals.

Namor

The amphibious Prince Namor grew up in the underwater kingdom of Atlantis. He is a super-fast swimmer and can communicate with marine life. Namor also has super strength and stamina, plus the ability to fly, thanks to small wings on his ankles.

At first Namor hated everyone who lived above the water, but he soon changed his mind and even joined forces with the Avengers.

Namor grows weaker the longer he is out of water.

Spider-Man and Wolverine

The current line up of the Avengers includes two very different Super Heroes —the amazing, web-slinging Spider-Man and the sharp-clawed, hard fighting Wolverine. Along with heroes such as Iron Man and Captain America, they have joined forces to keep the planet safe.

Spider-Man and Wolverine's powers complement each other. While Spidey brings stealth and agility to the team, Wolverine brings power and aggression.

Cold Front
Even Super Heroes feel the cold! Spider-Man and Wolverine brave sub-zero temperatures and blinding snow storms to save the day once again.

Daredevil

When young Matt Murdock saw a blind man about to be hit by a truck, he rushed to save him. Although the pedestrian was unhurt, some radioactive material fell from the truck and hit Matt in the face. The accident blinded Matt but somehow it also enhanced his other senses to Super Hero levels.

Matt learned to control his super powers and later adopted a secret costumed identity as the crime-fighting Daredevil.

Matt Murdock
By day Matt Murdock fights crime as a successful lawyer. At night he brings New York City's criminals to justice in a different way, as the masked Super Hero Daredevil.

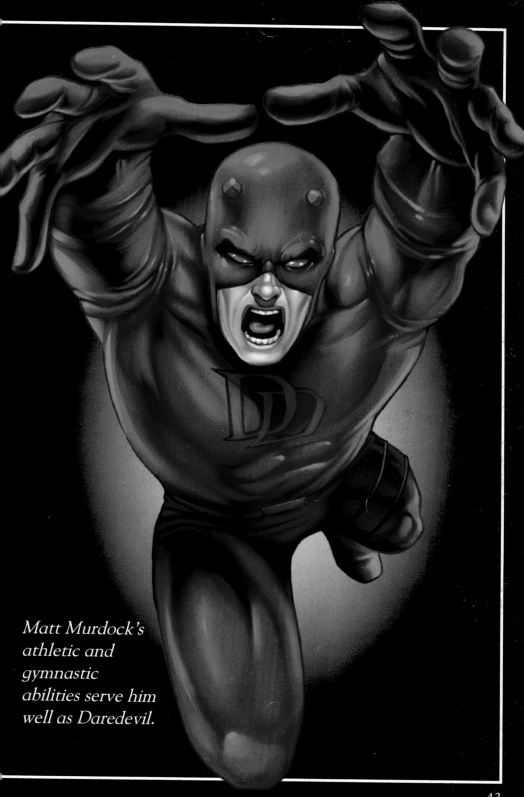

Matt Murdock's athletic and gymnastic abilities serve him well as Daredevil.

Elektra

Elektra Natchios' life changed when her father was killed during a hostage incident. She became a much angrier person and also began to train in martial arts. She learned how to use weapons such as the fearsome ninja sai and eventually became an assassin for hire.

Elektra is a skilled assassin. As well as her martial arts skills, she is a talented gymnast and possesses some telepathic powers. Few villains stand a chance against Elektra.

Kingpin
Elektra worked as a hired assassin for Wilson Fisk, the self-styled "Kingpin" of organised crime in New York City.

Daredevil and Elektra

Matt Murdock and Elektra Natchios fell in love when they were students at Columbia University in New York City. However, the relationship ended when Elektra's father was killed.

Elektra didn't come back into Matt's life until she started working as an assassin for Kingpin. Elektra's work for the crime boss put her in opposition to her one-time love, who was now the powerful crime-fighting Super Hero Daredevil.

However, when Elektra was mortally wounded by the evil Super Villain Bullseye, she sought out Matt one last time. Elektra died in Matt's arms but was later brought back to life by a villain called the Hand.

Glossary

Aggression
A hostile, angry, or destructive outlook on life.

Agility
The ability to move quickly, easily, and gracefully.

Alter ego
A side of someone's personality that is different, such as a secret identity.

Amphibious
Able to live both on land and in water.

Cosmic
Relating to the whole universe, not just planet Earth.

Endurance
The ability to withstand physical and, sometimes, mental, pressures.

Force field
An invisible protective barrier that cannot be penetrated by weapons or bad guys.

Gauntlet
A protective glove.

Martial arts
Oriental forms of combat, such as karate. Martial arts can also be practiced as sports.

Mutant
A human born with extraordinary features or special powers.

Radiation
Energy emitted in the form of waves or particles.

Radioactive
A way of describing an element that spontaneously emits rays that are often harmful.

Solar energy
Power that comes from the sun.

Stealth
The ability to move quietly and cautiously to avoid being detected.

Super Hero
A man, woman, or alien with special powers and abilities. A Super Hero uses his or her powers for good—to protect innocent people and worlds and to fight evil.

Super Hero team
A group of Super Heroes who work together e.g. the Avengers, the X-Men, and the Fantastic Four. Super Heroes become even stronger when they work together.

Super Villain
Also a man, woman, or alien with special powers and abilities. However, a Super Villain uses his or her abilities for evil—to gain power and harm innocent people.

Telekinesis
The ability to move objects just with the powers of the mind.

Telepathy
The ability to read the thoughts and feelings of other people.

Teleport
To travel a great distance in an instant. This could be done with a machine or simply by disappearing from one place and then reappearing in another, a moment later. Only some Super Heroes can do this.